GRAVITY

JASON CHIN

ANDERSEN PRESS

GRAVITY

MAKES

OBJECTS

WITHOUT GRAVITY, EVERYTHING WOULD

THE MOON

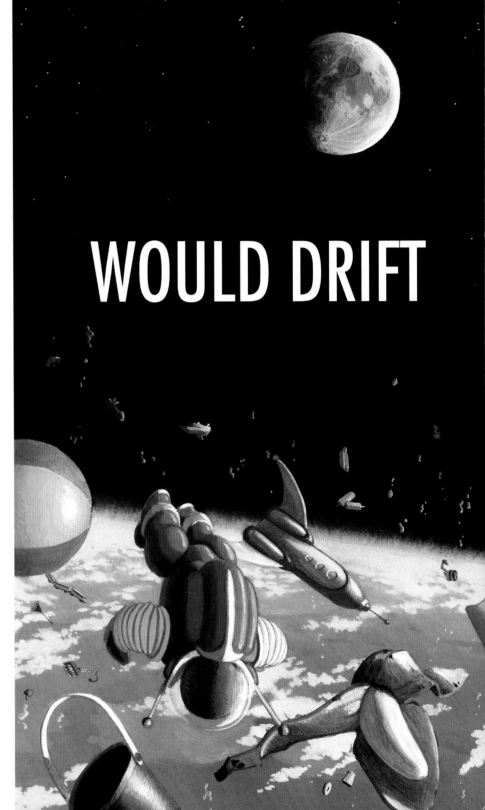

WOULD DRIFT

AWAY FROM

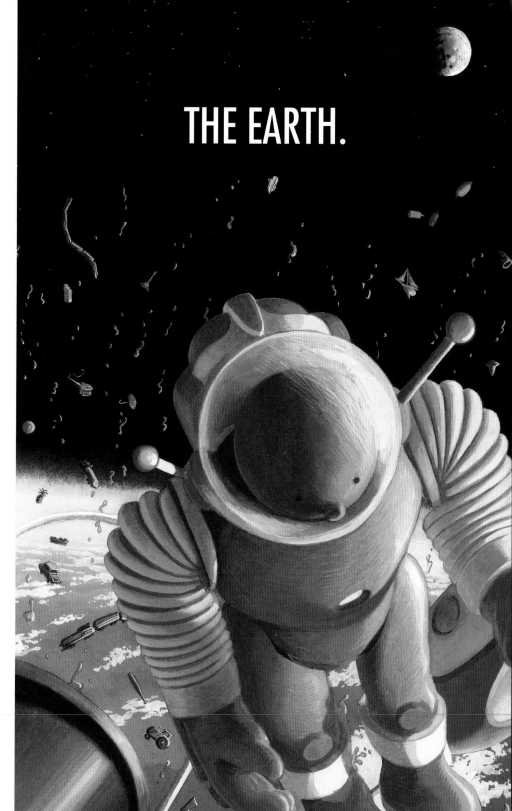

THE EARTH.

WOULD DRIFT

AWAY FROM

THE SUN.

LUCKILY, EVERYTHING
HAS GRAVITY.

MASSIVE THINGS HAVE A LOT OF GRAVITY . . .

AND THEIR GRAVITY PULLS ON SMALLER THINGS.

GRAVITY KEEPS
THE EARTH
NEAR THE SUN,

THE MOON
NEAR THE EARTH,

AND MAKES

OBJECTS FALL

TO EARTH.

MORE ABOUT GRAVITY

GRAVITY IS ATTRACTIVE

Gravity is an invisible force that causes objects to attract each other. Every object in the universe has gravity that is continuously pulling on every other object in the universe. When you jump into a pool, the Earth's gravity is what pulls you down towards the water.

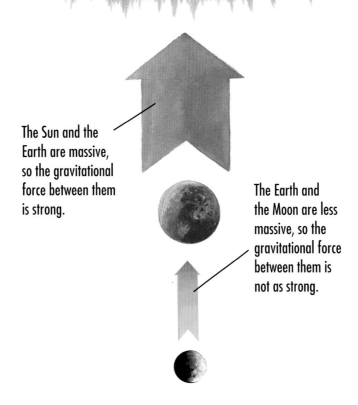

The Sun and the Earth are massive, so the gravitational force between them is strong.

The Earth and the Moon are less massive, so the gravitational force between them is not as strong.

WEAKER WITH DISTANCE

An object's gravity extends infinitely, but it becomes weaker with distance. Near its surface, Earth's gravity is strong enough to keep you on the ground, but millions of miles away, its gravity becomes so weak you wouldn't even notice it. Even though the gravity of all the stars in the universe is pulling on you, you can't feel it because they are much too far away.

Far from Earth, Earth's gravity is weak.

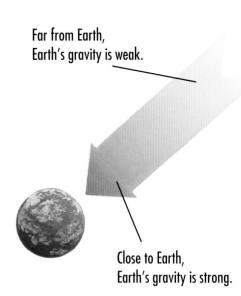

Close to Earth, Earth's gravity is strong.

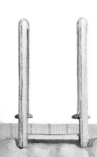

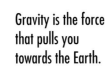

Gravity is the force that pulls you towards the Earth.

MORE MASS, MORE GRAVITY

The gravity pulling any two objects together is determined by the mass of both objects – the greater the combined mass, the stronger the gravity. For this reason, the force of gravity between the Earth and the Sun is stronger than the force of gravity between the Moon and the Earth.

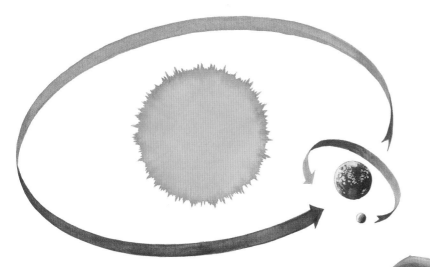

Gravity keeps the Earth in orbit around the Sun and the Moon in orbit around the Earth.

GRAVITY KEEPS IT ALL TOGETHER

The Earth travels around the Sun in a path called an *orbit*, and gravity keeps the Earth in this path. Imagine you have a ball on a string and you swing it in a circle. The string will keep the ball from flying away. The Sun's gravity is like the string: it keeps the Earth from flying away. All of the planets in our solar system orbit the Sun, and the Moon orbits the Earth, and gravity is what keeps the system together.

MASS MATTERS

Mass is the amount of *matter* (or "stuff") that makes up an object. Mass can be measured by weighing objects – heavier objects have more mass. Often, larger objects have more mass than smaller objects, but mass is not the same as size. A big box of air has less mass than a small box of bricks because there is more matter in the box of bricks.

Elephants weigh more than mice because they have more mass.

THE MEASURE OF GRAVITY

Weight is the measure of Earth's gravity pulling on objects. Since mass determines the amount of gravitational pull on an object, objects with more mass weigh more. Take an elephant and a mouse, for example. The elephant has more mass, so the gravitational pull on it is stronger, and since the pull on it is stronger, it weighs more than the mouse.

The string keeps the ball from flying away, similar to how gravity keeps the Earth from flying away from the Sun.

Dedicated to Allison, Maggie, Natalie and Molly

Thanks to Ralph Gibson,
Department of Physics and Astronomy, Dartmouth College

First published in Great Britain in 2014 by Andersen Press Ltd.,
20 Vauxhall Bridge Road, London SW1V 2SA.
Published in Australia by Random House Australia Pty.,
Level 3, 100 Pacific Highway, North Sydney, NSW 2060.
Published by arrangement with Roaring Brook Press,
a division of Holtzbrinck Publishing Holdings Limited Partnership.

10   9   8   7   6   5   4   3   2   1

British Library Cataloguing in Publication Data available.   ISBN 978 1 78344 197 6

BIBLIOGRAPHY

Branley, Franklyn M. *Gravity is a Mystery.* HarperCollins, 2007.

Breithaupt, Jim. *Teach Yourself Physics.* McGraw-Hill, 2003.

Crowther, J. G. *Six Great Scientists: Copernicus, Galileo, Newton, Darwin, Marie Curie, Einstein.* Barnes & Noble, 1995.

De Pree, Christopher G., Ph.D. *Physics Made Simple.* Broadway Books, 2004.

Gibilisco, Stan. *Advanced Physics Demystified.* McGraw-Hill, 2007.

Gleick, James. *Isaac Newton.* Vintage, 2004.

Krauss, Lawrence M. *Fear of Physics.* Basic Books, 2007.

White, Michael. *Isaac Newton: The Last Sorcerer.* Basic Books, 1999.